Macbeth

About the Author

Beverley Birch grew up in Kenya and first came to England, where she now lives with her husband and two daughters, at the age of fifteen. After completing an MA in Economics and Sociology, Beverley became an editor at Penguin. Within a few weeks she was offered the chance to work on children's books and has been involved in children's publishing – as both editor and writer – ever since.

She has had over forty books published, from picture books and novels to science biographies and retellings of classic works. All her titles have received critical acclaim and her work has been translated into more than a dozen languages. Her latest novel for teenagers, *Rift*, was published in 2006.

Shakespeare's Tales

Macbeth

Retold by Beverley Birch

Illustrated by Peter Chesterton

WAYLAND

For my mother, with love

Text copyright © 1988 Beverley Birch
Illustrations copyright © 2006 Peter Chesterton

First published in *Shakespeare's Stories: Tragedies* in 1988 by
Macdonald & Co (Publishers) Limited.
This edition first published in 2006 by
Wayland, an imprint of Hachette Children's Books

Cover and text design: Rosamund Saunders

Hachette Children's Books
338 Euston Road, London NW1 3BH

Printed and bound in the United Kingdom

ISBN-10: 0 7502 4965 X
ISBN-13: 978 0 7502 4965 2

The Cast

The Witches

King Duncan – King of Scotland

Malcolm – Duncan's son

Donalbain – Duncan's son

Macbeth – King Duncan's General

Banquo – King Duncan's General

Lady Macbeth – Macbeth's Wife

Macduff – the Thane of Fife,
a Scottish Lord

Sunless mists turned about the place, and rocks crouched low beneath a rumbling thunder. Into the circle of the gloom they came, twisting figures woven in the air, and with them came dark whisperings:

'When shall we three meet again, in thunder, lightning or in rain?'

Hoarse with a poisonous hate, the answer lingered.

'When the hurlyburly's done; when the battle's lost … and won.'

The sodden earth began to tremble …

'That will be before the set of sun.'

'Where the place?'

'Upon the heath.' A curdling wail rose through the air, as though a thousand wretched creatures were imprisoned in that moaning place.

'There to meet with *Macbeth*!' The final venomous shriek swept from the writhing shadows low across the heather and then up, up into the eye of a blackly gathering storm …

King Duncan's camp was bright and quick with movement. Men strode fast between low flickering fires and every hour the messengers sped from the battlefield towards the waiting king.

A soldier stumbled into camp, staggered, and fell. They saw the staring horror of a long-fought battle in his face and ropes of blood draining his filth-streaked limbs.

They raised him up and sent for
dressings for his wounds, while
battle-weary men gathered around.

Between hoarse, panting breaths the
soldier spilled his tale: how bitterly the
battle ebbed and flowed! Neither the
soldiers of the king nor those of the
rebel army were gaining ground, until …
his voice broke, sobbed, and listeners
drew closer, fearing the worst. It seemed
the villainous rebel Macdonwald gained
a hold and viciously pressed forward his
attack! And then …

'Brave Macbeth! Well he deserves
that name!' the soldier cried, and a new
fire coursed through his limbs, as
with his arms swung wide he showed

the mighty swordsweeps of Macbeth.
His listeners could almost see Macbeth
carve his unflinching path through
spear and axe.

'At last,' he said, 'Macbeth stood face to
face against Macdonwald.' And now the
soldier stood erect, as though he would
draw Macbeth's great strength into his
own battered limbs. And with gigantic
swirling blows he showed how Macbeth
battled Macdonwald towards his death. A
mighty, final deathstroke the soldier gave,
and there, before the watchers' eyes, the
rebel Macdonwald fell.

'O valiant cousin!' King Duncan's voice
shook. How could his gratitude for
Macbeth's valour be weighed in words? It
seemed that Scotland's fate, the people's

lives, his own, were cradled in the vast courage of this warrior's breast.

'But mark, King of Scotland, mark,' the soldier swayed and a grey weariness drained his face. 'The King of Norway with new supplies of men began a fresh assault!'

'Did this dismay our generals, Macbeth and Banquo?' the King questioned urgently.

'Yes …' A sharp in-drawn breath hissed through the crowd. So the battle was now lost! The soldier drew up his trembling body and threw his shoulders wide. 'As sparrows would dismay the eagle or the hare dismay the lion!'

'Ah … ' the single murmur of relief swept around, with nods and smiles. Even

12

now they could see Macbeth and Banquo fighting stroke for stroke against the enemy, their demon onslaught drawing other soldiers on with new-born strength! But now the soldier who told the tale grew faint, and sank to the ground.

'Your wounds tell of your honour, as do your words,' King Duncan said. 'Go, get him to the surgeons.'

He swung suddenly on his heel as a new commotion sounded at the gate. It was the Thane of Ross, hot-foot from the battlefield. He sped through the camp towards them. 'God save the King!' he cried. 'The King of Norway himself, helped by that disloyal traitor the Thane of Cawdor, began a dismal conflict! Until our general, Macbeth,

like the unvanquished God of War,
confronted him sword point against
point, arm against arm … ' The
thane's voice soared with triumph,
'and, to conclude, the victory fell on us!'

'Great happiness!' King Duncan's voice
broke. He raised his arms silently, as
though to encircle every loyal man. The
bloody course of battle was now run and
all the rebels were in flight. His aged
shoulders straightened, as though finally
he threw off a weighty burden.

What rich rewards he owed to loyal
men! He sighed: so too he owed
punishment to the rebel lord who
joined with an invading king.

Swiftly he gave commands. Traitors
would no more betray this land: *death*

would be the payment for that Thane of Cawdor's treachery.

'And with the traitor's title,' triumphantly the king announced, 'greet Macbeth.' His voice grew sombre. 'What Cawdor has lost, noble Macbeth has won!' With these words King Duncan's hand rose up, slowly, as though the great Macbeth were cradled in his royal grasp.

Storm clouds swelled above the heath. The last rim of light lingered, hopelessly, and then was smothered.

At the crossroads, the air grew heavy. Gorsebushes and blackened tree stumps trembled. Darkness sank, thick and dark

15

and oily; and from its centre a reeking vapour coiled, snaked upward from the earth, spiralled and spread …

Within, three figures moved: twisted forms of wizened skin and knotted hair. Locked one to the other in a grimly rhythmic sway they turned, now this way, now the other, the murmur of their chant like some fiendish heartbeat in the rising howl of winds.

Above the gale a drumbeat boomed. The figures paused, and swivelled towards the sound and a glow of ugly glee inflamed their watching faces.

Macbeth and Banquo trod a weary path across the heath, and with resounding drumbeat Banquo killed the memories of horror on the field of war.

Macbeth walked deep in thought. He shrugged his shoulders high against the winds.

Banquo's drumbeat stopped. Into their faces rose a stench as though a rottenness steamed from the caverns of a poisonous earth. Three withered forms rose to their gaze: gnarled skeletons of rag and bone sheathed in a bloody light. Each raised a crooked finger to skinny lips. Macbeth shivered. An iciness seeped through his bones. He summoned all his will.

'Speak if you can! What are you?' His command rose into the wind.

One grisly figure rasped a crackling chant:

'All hail Macbeth! hail to thee, Thane of Glamis!'

17

Another, 'All hail, Macbeth! hail to thee, Thane of Cawdor!'

The words hung in the rancid air. In that moment, waiting, Macbeth felt a coiling in his stomach, as though a serpent writhed …

'All hail, Macbeth! that shalt be king hereafter!'

In the warrior's heart there was a hammering as though his ribs would break. King!

To be king!

Banquo moved towards the apparitions. 'If you can look into the seeds of time, and say which grain will grow, and which will not, speak then to me … '

'Hail!' the creaking voices rose to a crescendo.

'Lesser than Macbeth, and greater.'

'Not so happy, yet much happier.'

'Thou shalt get kings, though thou be none!'

Macbeth broke across their rhythm. 'Tell me more: I know I am Thane of Glamis; but how of Cawdor? The Thane of Cawdor lives … ' he paused, 'and to be king …' It was beyond belief. How could they know? What more might they foresee?

'Speak!' he cried, more urgently, but already the gory glow that held the monstrous trio began to seep into the sodden ground; their forms began to melt. Only the odour of decay hung in the leaden air.

Macbeth and Banquo were alone again.

'Your children shall be kings,' murmured Macbeth.

'*You* shall be king,' Banquo's voice betrayed the wonder of his half-belief.

Macbeth's thoughts churned. There *is* a king; there *is* a Thane of Cawdor. The storm shrieked the words into a thundering pattern inside his head.

'Who's here?' At Banquo's sudden cry, two men broke through the gloom towards them, breathless with the burden of their news: the fame of Macbeth's battle deeds had reached the king and they now brought the monarch's thanks to him.

And yet their words were almost lost, for he was hearing other voices in the wind. Until the words '*the Thane of Cawdor*' pierced his thoughts: the Thane of Cawdor had been judged a traitor, and as thanks for Macbeth's services in war, and sign of honours yet to come, the king *now gave Macbeth that name.*

The prophecy! Already one part true.

What of the other part? Before his eyes there rose an image of the king. Bold, strong, alive.

Yet *I* should be king. The hammering in his ribs grew stronger. Hair rose across his scalp, as though some dreadful thought was searching for a nesting place within his brain.

And yet, the image was already there.

The vision of a single, bloody act.

To kill the king.

The thought swelled, and became alive, and Macbeth struggled to push it back.

21

'Come friends,' he forced himself to say, 'let us towards the king … '

In the palace the king awaited news. Had Cawdor been executed yet? The business troubled him.

'He was a gentleman on whom I built an absolute trust,' he murmured to Malcolm, his son. He sighed: how little of what a person really thought was written on their face! He grew weary with this sorrow; his trust had been so painfully misplaced.

There was a sudden commotion in the Court and cries of jubilant welcome. Macbeth and Banquo had come! The king rose swiftly to meet them: such true men they were, throwing their lives

behind their loyalty to Scotland and
her king!

'O worthiest cousin!' his heart
overflowed with all he owed Macbeth:
more, more than ever he could pay.

Macbeth stood, great and battle-stained
before his king.

'Our duties,' he paused, beating back a
thousand whirling thoughts, 'our duties
are to your throne and state. We do only
what we should, by doing everything to
ensure your safety, love and honour.'

For a long, silent moment, the king
grasped his hand. 'Welcome! You are
welcome here!'

And now he turned to Macbeth's
staunch companion.

'Noble Banquo! You have deserved no

less.' Warmly he embraced his general, and turned away to wipe the joyful tears which now flowed freely down his cheeks.

Then he swung with sudden resolution to face the waiting Court. 'Sons, kinsmen, thanes,' he said, steadying his voice, 'know that I now declare as heir to my throne and state … '

Macbeth looked up, a quickening pulse beating below his temple. So soon! The final prophecy!

And yet the king was moving past and placing a hand upon the shoulder of his son!

' … my eldest, Malcolm. We name him heir to the throne and Prince of Cumberland.'

A mist of whispering thoughts leapt to

Macbeth's brain. He was not to be the future king, but the king's son, Malcolm, would be instead!

That is a step, he breathed, on which I must fall down, or else … he searched for his answer, and a restless anguish coiled within him: the serpent of ambition writhed – he recognized it fully now. He saw the crown on Duncan's head burning as a beacon to draw him on. He *would* be king.

'Stars, hide your fires. Let not light see my black and deep desires.'

The lady lifted the letter to the flickering light and read again. A strange tale, her lord Macbeth told her! Bewitched encounters on the heath; glorious

honours foretold. The letter breathed
fire into her very limbs, and answered
an inward flame.

She seemed to see her husband
stand before her, tall and strong.

'Glamis you are, and Cawdor,' she
murmured, 'and you shall be what you
are promised.'

And yet, she saw him too, too clearly.
'I do fear your nature. It is too full of the
milk of human kindness.' How well she
knew that! He wanted greatness, power,
wealth; but would not willingly play falsely
for it. He yearned for that which was not
his; and yet he would not do what *must* be
done, to win.

'Macbeth,' she longed to see him.
'Hurry to me, that I may pour my

courage in your ear ...' There was a sudden movement at the door. A messenger! She turned urgently to hear his news.

'The king comes here tonight,' he said.

'Tonight!' She signalled him away and turned, to gaze far into the distance beyond the castle walls.

Tonight! She closed her eyes. Deep within her lungs, her stomach, her loins, she drew breath, as though she would suck the fires from the centre of the earth.

'Come you spirits that wait on human thoughts,' she cried, 'fill me from crown to toe top-full of direst cruelty! Make thick my blood ... come, come, thick night ... '

Tonight they would begin the climb

towards the crown. Tonight they would kill the king. She saw the crown now shining only for them …

It was there Macbeth found her, and wordlessly they clung together.

'My dearest love,' he murmured then, not looking in her eyes, 'Duncan comes here tonight,' and he turned restlessly to avoid her gaze.

She seized his face and swung it towards her, and her hand was steel.

'You shall put this night's business into my care.'

Hastily Macbeth drew back from her, lowering his eyes. 'We will speak further.'

'Only look up!' she urged. 'Leave all the rest to me!'

The royal party came at dusk: the king and his two sons, Malcolm and Donalbain; Banquo and all the noble lords. Their mood was light. The fruits of victory against the enemy were now secured, and it gave to all of them a pleasant lack of care. They marvelled at the sweet summer air that flowed so softly about Macbeth's castle. And how warmly did his lady welcome them into her home! Words of honour and loving debt flowed from her lips, and in the evening she prepared a sumptuous banquet for her royal guests.

It pleased King Duncan well. The castle halls rang with the joyful sound of music; servants flew to and fro; great dishes steamed with the rich odours of succulent foods and torches flamed a merry welcome.

Only Macbeth left the festivities, suddenly, and sought the dark. Alone in the courtyard, he strode to and fro.

What visions bedevilled his tired brain! If only such deeds as he imagined could be swiftly done, and ended there. But could there ever be rest again after the murder of a king? Could there ever be sleep again after the killing of a man so gracious, noble, kind, as Duncan?

'He's here in double trust,' he told himself. 'First, as I am his cousin and his subject; and then, as I am his host, who should shut the door against his murderer, not bear the knife myself.'

And yet the serpent coiled within him
still. To be king! To rule all Scotland!

Lady Macbeth came searching for
him, angrily.

'We'll go no further in this business,'
he said to her.

Such scorn she spat at him, he winced
beneath its lash!

'Are you afraid?'

'Peace,' Macbeth struggled against
her rage. 'I dare do all that is fitting for
a man.'

'What beast was it then, that made you
break this enterprise to me? When you
dared do it, *then* you were a man!'

He strove to find another reason
against the deed: 'If we should fail?'

'We fail! But screw your courage to

the sticking place and we'll not fail!' She stood before him, certain in her power. And step by step, she laid her deadly plan before him: Duncan's servant would be overpowered with wine and fall into a drunken stupor. 'What cannot you and I perform upon the unguarded Duncan then?'

Her certainties lulled him. The bloody visions stilled.

It was all settled, now.

They stood together, each with a private vision of the golden promises to come. Each bone and sinew must be steeled and bent to do this horrible thing. Macbeth prepared.

He waited, shrouded in the darkness of the court. The revelry was over and all the guests were in bed; Macbeth alone listened for the bell to call him to the night's grim task.

How long those minutes were until that dread bell's note!

He looked into the shadows, moving with an uneasy tread. And then he halted, staring, aghast.

'Is this a dagger which I see before me, the handle towards my hand?' He tried to seize the weapon, but his fingers passed through air. And still the blade hung there!

And now it dripped with blood!

He stumbled back against the stair

that led towards the king.

'There's no such thing,' he cried. 'It is this bloody business which brings it to my eyes!'

Against the wall, he felt the hardness of the stone along his back. This wall was real. So was the earth on which he stood. He braced himself and stilled his trembling mind.

The bell! Far off it tolled. The summons from his wife coursed through his body like a fire, and drew him on, on up the stair, towards the sleeping king …

His wife came into the blanketing gloom within the court. She had drunk some of the wine that she had given to King Duncan's guards and it had fired her inward flame.

She was now ready.

She strained her ears towards the rooms beyond the stairs.

'He is about it.'

She listened again. 'I laid their daggers ready; he could not miss them!' But what if the guards awoke before Macbeth had killed the king? She raised her hands against her face. They trembled, and she had not known they would.

She thought then of the king, asleep, at peace, as she had seen him only a few moments ago, and a sudden ache stirred through her. 'Had he not looked like my father as he slept, I would have done it.'

A shuffling lurch came on the stair above! Macbeth swayed there, ashen-faced.

'I have done the deed,' he whispered. 'Did you not hear a noise?'

'I heard the owl scream and the crickets cry,' she answered him. 'Did you not speak?'

'When?'

'Now.'

'As I descended?' he searched the darkness beyond her.

'Ay,' she moved towards him.

He pulled away and stared at his bloody hands. 'This is a sorry sight.'

'A foolish thought to say a sorry sight!' she retorted angrily.

He raised his eyes and looked into her face, and what eyes they were!

And then he froze, as though somewhere within the winds that gathered round their towers he'd heard a sound. He pointed a trembling finger, 'I thought I heard a voice cry "Sleep no more, Macbeth has murdered sleep."'

'What do you mean?' she cried.

He stumbled to the window, 'Still it cried, "Sleep no more! … Glamis has murdered sleep, and therefore Cawdor shall sleep no more; Macbeth shall sleep no more!"'

She seized his arm, and she was scornful now.

'Go, get some water and wash this filthy witness from your hand.' In horror she seized the blades clutched in his fingers. 'Why did you bring these daggers from the place? They must lie there: go carry them.'

'I'll go no more!' Macbeth gasped, hoarse. 'I am afraid to think what I have done. Look on it again, I dare not.'

'Give me the daggers!' She sped up the stairs. And if the king was bleeding, why, she would smear his blood across the guards and everyone would see that it was they who had done this thing!

A thunderous knocking boomed across the court. Macbeth shuddered, and did not move.

'What hands are here? They pluck out my eyes! All great Neptune's ocean will not wash this blood clean from my hand!'

She had returned, and now her hands too reeked with Duncan's blood! He recoiled in horror as she held them up. 'My hands are of your colour, but I shame

to wear a heart so white!' she said.

Again the knocking thundered. She urged his attention, pulling him towards their rooms. 'A little water clears us of this deed. How easy it is then!' The knocking came again. 'Hark! Get on your nightgown.'

As though he saw the hammer of doom beyond, Macbeth stared wretchedly at the outer door. 'Wake Duncan with this knocking! I wish you could!'

It was Macduff, the noble Thane of Fife who came with other lords to wake the king. They hammered at the castle door and shivered in the bitter morning chill. How warm the summer bloom of evening air had been the night before;

and yet what storms had torn the sky since then! The wind had seemed to scream with agony, and trembling, like a fever, shook the earth.

Macbeth greeted them, dressed in his nightgown and told them the king was not yet up.

'I'll bring you to him,' Macbeth said.

He led Macduff towards the room. The thane went in. There was a moment as he crossed the floor, a pause, a strangled gasp, and then a cry that pierced the very stones around them.

'O horror, horror, horror! Awake, awake!' Macduff's voice rang throughout the castle. 'Murder and treason! Banquo and Donalbain! Malcolm! Awake!'

Bells rang, torches flamed and the

castle echoed with running feet.

Lady Macbeth hurried to them: what hideous thing had so alarmed her guests?

'Our royal master's murdered!'

Who? Who had done it? His guards! Bathed in the king's blood, confused and babbling, their filthy daggers lying on their pillows.

But Macbeth, in fury for the murder of his king, it seemed, had taken swift revenge and killed them instantly!

'Why did you do so?' Macduff exclaimed. It startled him. So swiftly to kill those they could question about the night's unnatural events: their punishment was too hastily done!

Or was it? A grain was seeded in Macduff's mind, even as he heard the words of grief spilling from Macbeth's lips. He watched him. And Lady Macbeth watched Macduff.

Could this bold thane already see the lies that lurked below the surface of her husband's words? Did he suspect Macbeth had killed the guards to stop them talking?

'Help me!' she swayed, as though about to faint.

'Look to the lady,' Macduff commanded. They rushed to help her. And no one else, it seemed, had seen what he had seen.

Within the hour Malcolm and Donalbain sped from the castle. It seemed to Malcolm that the murderer of a king would turn next to the murder of the sons and heirs to that king's throne. Here, for them, there were daggers in men's smiles.

The dark spirits of the heath had sowed their poisonous seed and what rich soil it had found! How it had grown and fruited!

And now the crop was nearly in: King Duncan dead and Malcolm, the heir to the throne, in flight. It seemed to everyone that it must prove his guilt: he must have bribed the guards to murder his own father.

The nobles sought a new heir to the throne of Scotland. Macbeth! So loyal and honest a cousin to king Duncan; and had he not in battle proved his love for Scotland and her king?

And so Macbeth took up the crown, and no one could deny so worthy a man ascending to Duncan's royal seat.

Except Macduff, the noble Thane of Fife. He did not attend the coronation of Macbeth, but watched it from afar, and wondered.

Banquo remained, adviser to Macbeth. But such cursed thoughts he'd had since that dark day upon the heath, and such vile dreams now mocked his sleep!

He thought of the new-made king, Macbeth. 'You have it now,' he murmured. 'King, Cawdor, Glamis, all as the weird women promised, and I fear you played most foully for it.'

But had they not also said that he would be root and father of many kings? The promise beckoned him, and yet his nature struggled with the poison of the witches' words, and deep within, he knew how Macbeth had taken the crown …

Macbeth came to him, richly dressed in royal robes and attended by his queen, the lords and nobles of the Court. He announced, 'Tonight, we hold a ceremonial supper, sir, and I request your presence.'

'Let your highness command me,' Banquo replied. Each minute his distance from this man who was his friend seemed to get wider.

'Will you ride this afternoon?' Macbeth enquired. 'Is it far you ride?'

'As far, my lord, as will fill up the time between now and supper.'

The king nodded, thoughtfully. 'Fail not our feast.' And he watched Banquo go, taking his young son with him. This man now woke a fear in Macbeth's breast that clawed deep as a dagger's blade.

'There is no one but he whose being I do fear,' he thought. Brave, wise Banquo: he knew of the dark women on the heath, and of their promises. And had they not hailed him as father to a line of kings? 'To *me* they did not speak of heirs: no son will follow *me* on to the throne.'

The barren prospect chilled Macbeth with a new and terrifying pain. To have dredged up such evil from within his

49

soul; to have stilled all the warmth of loyalty, honour, love, humanity! And all for what?

'Then I have defiled my mind for Banquo's sons. For them I have murdered the gracious Duncan. For Banquo's heirs I have given up my soul to the dark spirits and surrendered sleep to the shuddering visions of these endless nights ... '

The agony worked deep within him, bending him towards new avenues of hate. He sent for cloaked, hidden men with scowling desperation on their faces. And in their hands Macbeth now laid the lives of Banquo and his son. This threat to him *would* end; snuffed like a candle even as they rode towards his feast.

51

And all the while the queen roamed listlessly. A drugging weariness now bedevilled every step she took. All had seemed so simple when she planned it: the crown was so near at hand, so easy for the taking, and the murder of a man so quick, so neatly done.

And yet what was it worth, now that they had it all?

'My lord, why do you keep alone?' she questioned Macbeth again. She ached to stand with him as once she had, when that shining thread of their ambition had woven them together. 'What's done is done,' she pleaded, but her words fell on stony ground.

'We have scorched the snake, not killed it,' he retorted sharply. Could she not see

the snake would return to rip his nights
with poisoned tooth?

These dreams that nightly tortured him!

'So full of scorpions is my mind, dear
wife!' he said to her.

'Gentle my love,' she tried to touch his
face. 'Be bright and jovial among your
guests tonight.'

I n a dark place near the palace
Macbeth's murderers did their swift
butcher's work and sliced the life
from Banquo.

But Banquo's son escaped and fled into
the night.

In the palace the ceremonial feast
was laid: a royal banquet to hail a
new-crowned king. Macbeth played

monarch with gracious words, welcoming his guests and preparing to drink a toast to them.

There was a sudden movement. The murderer came to the door with blood smeared on his face, and hastily Macbeth went to him.

Was Banquo dead? Yes, his throat was cut, and twenty deep gashes on his head. His son? His son had fled!

The fear swelled in Macbeth like the last wave that would drown him as he stood. He braced himself, and turned towards the celebration feast, summoning the smilings of a host on to his face. The lords hailed him to sit with them.

'The table's full,' he said. He could not see an empty place to sit. Even where they showed him there was a place, there was a man ...

But it was not a man! It was the tatters of a man, all gashed and soaked with blood, his head half-hanging from his gaping neck ... it stared at him, and stared ... Macbeth cried, 'You cannot say I did it. Never shake your gory locks at me!'

The nobles leapt in consternation to their feet; the queen urged them to sit again.

'Shame!' she hissed at trembling Macbeth. 'Why do you make such faces? When all's done, you look but on a stool!'

He looked, and it was gone. He straightened up and breathed again.

'The time has been that, when the

brains were out, the man would die, and there an end,' he assured the startled Court. 'But now they rise again and push us from our stools!'

The queen seized his arm. Had he lost all his sense? The nobles would hear and know what they had done! She urged him towards the feast. He strained to hold his mind and body firm, and once more he approached the table.

Again! Banquo! All pale and bloody, and staring with sightless eyes! He tried to shield himself, 'How can you behold such sights,' he accused the watching nobles, 'and keep the natural ruby of your cheeks when mine are blanched with fear?'

'What sights, my lord?' a thane enquired of him.

'I pray you, speak not,' the queen pleaded. 'He is not well. Question enrages him. Stand not upon the order of your going, but go at once!'

They went. But they had heard.

'It will have blood,' Macbeth murmured wretchedly. 'They say blood will have blood.'

His wife stood watching him. There was no life left in her now. All was spent. She saw how far beyond her reach he now had moved! Sleep beckoned her, only sleep. How long was it since she, or he, had slept?

Macbeth's brain fastened on a new thought. Macduff! He had not come to celebrate. Macduff refused to celebrate his kingship Macbeth knew, for did he not keep spies in every noble's court? Did he not need them to sniff out hidden treacheries that rose against a king! Fears pressed down on him from every side and hemmed him in. Suddenly he made up his mind. 'I will tomorrow, early, go to the weird sisters. More shall they speak, for now I am bent to know, by the worst means, the worst. For my own good, all others shall give way! I wade so deep in blood already that returning would be as wretched as going on!'

Now the strange behaviour of the king was known, and far and wide the people talked of it. They said that he was mad, and whispered of the bloody path by which he had mounted to the throne.

It was also known that Malcolm had received a royal welcome in England, at King Edward's court. There also Macduff, the Thane of Fife, had gone, to ask the English king for help. He said that Malcolm, the rightful heir to Duncan, should come against Macbeth, the murdering usurper of the royal throne of Scotland.

Macbeth learned of these moves against him, and prepared.

He found the twisted women of the heath in a deep cavern, brooding like vultures above a cauldron's steam. They swayed and moaned and threw some vile, rotting thing into the bilious brew, and grimly their chant rose above the cauldron's hiss.

'Round about the cauldron go
In the poisoned entrails throw.

Double, double toil and trouble;
Fire burn and cauldron bubble.

Fillet of a fenny snake.
In the cauldron boil and bake;
Eye of newt and toe of frog,
Wool of bat and tongue of dog …

Double, double toil and trouble;
Fire burn and cauldron bubble.'

'How now, you secret, black and midnight hags!' he cried. 'I conjure you, answer me!'

To his command there came a crash of thunder. From the cauldron rose a helmeted head which opened bloodless lips and spoke:

61

'Macbeth! Macbeth! Beware Macduff.
Beware the Thane of Fife!'

The vision sank. His fears were real!
Thunder rolled again, and now an
infant hovered above the cauldron's
stench, its body and its tiny limbs all
stained with blood as though new born.
It spoke!

'Be bloody, bold and resolute;
laugh to scorn the power of man,
for none of woman born shall
harm Macbeth.'

His heart surged with new hope.
'Then live, Macduff: Why need I
fear you? You had a mother who
gave birth to you, as do we all …
And yet … he would kill him, just
to be sure, just to strangle these

swarming terrors.

Thunder again: the image of a child that wore a crown and held a branch towards him.

'Be lion-mettled, proud,' the vision spoke. 'Macbeth shall never vanquished be until great Birnam Wood to high Dunsinane Hill shall come against him.'

His courage soared. Safe! Safe! How could a wood take up its roots and move? The rebellion raised against him in England could never win. Not until the wood at Birnam moved! He laughed to think of it.

'Yet my heart throbs to know one thing,' he questioned urgently. 'Shall Banquo's descendants ever reign in this kingdom?'

The cauldron sank into the ground, and now there came a line of kings: one, two, three, … each one with Banquo's face, and the vision burned his eyes out, for their crowns shone like the sun itself … six, seven, and in a mirror the eighth one showed him a score of others gliding after … And all the while the bloody Banquo smiled and smiled and showed they were all his!

Macbeth fell to his knees, covering his face. All this vast sea of evil he had steeped his being in, and yet it would be Banquo's descendants on the throne, not his …

Round about the fallen figure the withered women danced.

Suddenly he was alone. He stumbled to

his feet. Gone? 'Damned be all those that trust them,' he cried.

There seemed no end to Scotland's wounds. The country sank beneath the yoke of an enraged and corrupted king: it wept, it bled, and each new day a gash was added to the festering wounds. His villainies seemed to taint the very air that Scotland's people breathed.

At first, Macbeth plotted Macduff's death. But then he learned Macduff had reached England, and as if no evil was now beyond his fevered grasp, he ordered instead the deaths of all who could be found inside the castle of Macduff!

The children, wife, the servants of
the Thane of Fife – all put to the knife
by Macbeth's murderers.

But good men began to gather against
his tyranny. Macbeth went to the great
castle at high Dunsinane to prepare for
war, and with him went the queen.

But she was no longer like the queen.
She was a shadow, pale and lifeless,
except when she walked by night, asleep.

Her gentlewoman fetched the doctor to
see what illness could so shake the queen
that she would leave her bed and wander
in the echoing halls, would make her
always keep a candle by her side as
though she shrank from some dark
menace in the night.

They waited secretly for her. There

came the flicker of her candle, and the wasted figure of the queen moved into sight. She walked as in a trance, rubbing her thin white hands as though she washed them, but with such violence as if she tried to rip the skin from every bone.

'Yet here's a spot,' she gasped. 'Out, out, damned spot! Out I say!' She shuddered: but she could see the blood was on them still!

She thought she saw her husband stand before her now, as once he was. 'Fie, my lord, fie! A soldier, and afraid! What need we fear who knows it?' She searched the dark, and sobbed, 'Who would have thought the old man to have had so much blood in him?' And she half sang, 'The Thane of Fife had a wife.

Where is she now?'

Her trembling hands rose before her face.

'What, will these hands never be clean? Here's the smell of blood still.' And with a long, piteous sigh, she sobbed, 'All the perfumes of Arabia will not sweeten this little hand.'

Suddenly she stood tall and shook her head reproachfully.

'Wash your hands, put on your nightgown. Look not so pale. I tell you yet again Banquo's buried; he cannot come out of his grave.'

The listeners heard, aghast. Now the source of madness in the queen, was clear!

'Look after her,' the doctor urged. 'Remove from her the means of all

harm to herself and always keep your eyes on her.'

Not far from Dunsinane the Scottish lords were gathering, and even men close to Macbeth now went to lend their strength to Malcolm's cause. They prepared to meet the English force with Malcolm and Macduff near Birnam Wood.

Macbeth fortified Dunsinane. But what need he fear these armies massing against him? Could Birnam Wood ever move to Dunsinane? 'Never! Macduff was born of woman; no man born of woman shall ever have power over me, so said the women of the heath!'

But still there was no rest for him.

He reeled with tiredness and an inward, festering wound that turned all sour.

'I'll fight,' he cried, with sudden, savage rage. 'I'll fight till from my bones my flesh be hacked. Give me my armour!'

'It is not needed yet,' they told him.

'I'll put it on! Send out more horses; scour the country round; hang all those that talk of fear! Give me my armour!' And then, 'Pull it off, I say.' He flung the servant from him.

The English and the Scottish armies met at Birnam Wood. Malcolm surveyed the host of men joined with him against the tyrant and he was proud. 'Let every soldier cut down a branch and bear it before him,' he commanded. 'So shall we hide our numbers from Macbeth.'

Within the castle Macbeth gave commands. 'Hang out our banners on the outward walls.'

A sudden cry came from the inner rooms, a wail so stark, and desolate and chill it should have iced him to his heart. But what was one more desolation, one more horror to him now?

His servant brought the news.

'The queen, my lord, is dead.'

Macbeth turned away. What a vacant, futile life this was, when all was done. The future and the past yawned with arid emptiness on either side of him.

'Tomorrow and tomorrow and tomorrow creep in this petty pace from day to day to the last syllable of recorded time.' He searched for the purpose in it, but there was none. 'Life's but a tale told by an idiot, full of sound and fury, signifying nothing … '

A messenger burst in on him. 'As I stood watch upon the hill I looked towards Birnam and I thought the wood began to move!'

A dark, ravaging terror took Macbeth. Fear not, the fiends had said, till Birnam Wood do come to Dunsinane.

And now it came.

He thrust the terror from him. 'Arm, arm and out. Ring the alarms. Blow wind, come wrack! At least we'll die with armour on our back!'

Beyond the fortress walls the drums of Malcolm's soldiers boomed and trumpets called to war. 'Throw down your leafy screens,' Malcolm commanded his men. 'Show yourselves as those you are!'

Macbeth came from the fortress, fighting, scorning all. One final prophecy was yet to come. 'The fiends have tied me to a stake,' he cried, 'I cannot fly, but like a bear I must fight the course! What's he that was not born of woman? Such a one am I to fear, or none!'

Great Dunsinane surrendered to Malcolm's force. Now Duncan's son and heir strode through the gates as victor of the day.

Macduff sought Macbeth everywhere. He blistered for the lives of all his

murdered children, wife, and all. He
burned for Scotland's wrongs.

'Turn, hell-hound, turn!' he cried.

Macbeth turned, and faced the great
Macduff: traitor against royal thane.
A full circle the wheel had come, since
he, Macbeth, loyal thane, had faced
the traitors once. It seemed as though
all the evil of his poisonous days
now menaced him in this one man.

'Get back,' he urged. 'My soul is
weighed too heavily already with your
blood. Get back!'

'I have no words, my voice is in
my sword.' Macduff defied him, and
leapt forward.

Macbeth held him at bay. 'I bear a
charmed life,' he panted, 'which must

not yield to one of woman born.'

'Then despair,' Macduff cried, 'and let the demons that have guided you tell you that I, Macduff, was ripped from my mother's womb before my time!'

So, the last twisted fruit of bitter evil was now plucked. How they had played with him, those sisters of the heath, with double talk and circling promises that lead him ever on towards false hope! And how he had fed and nurtured their poison.

But he had reached the end. And as if to redeem the broken promise of his once glorious life, he surged towards Macduff; as though by fighting he would again draw through his veins all the honour, courage and warmth that once he'd had.

But Macbeth's time was done, as was his queen's. Macduff it was that plucked his life away and drew off the poison in the land. In killing Macbeth he gave Scotland back her rightful line of kings. And with great Macbeth's death, tyranny was dead; the vicious flame of murder, treachery and disorder in the land was quenched.

Macduff bowed low before Malcolm, Prince of Cumberland. 'Hail, King of Scotland! The time is free.'